JAN 2014

SPEED MACHINES

ASTON MARTIN

Julia J. Quinlan

PowerKiDS press

New York

Published in 2014 by The Rosen Publishing Group, Inc.
29 East 21st Street, New York, NY 10010

First Edition

Editor: Jennifer Way
Book Design: Greg Tucker
Book Layout: Kate Vlachos

Photo Credits: Cover, pp. 11, 14, 21 Max Earey/Shutterstock.com; p. 4 EML/Shutterstock.com; p. 5 TanArt/Shutterstock.com; pp. 6–7 Maxim Blinkov/Shutterstock.com; p. 8 Tim Graham/Tim Graham Photo Library/Getty Images; p. 9 © Transtock/ SuperStock; p. 10 dutourdumonde/Shutterstock.com; p. 11 (top) KENCKOphotography/Shutterstock.com; p. 12 Adam Middleton/Shutterstock.com; p. 13 Darrell Ingham/Getty Images Sport/Getty Images; p. 15 esbobeldijk/Shutterstock.com; p. 16 Manchester Daily Express/SSPL/Getty Images; p. 17 Stan Honda/AFP/Getty Images; pp. 18–19 Maurice Volmeyer/ Shutterstock.com; p. 20 Ben Smith/Shutterstock.com; pp. 22, 26, 28 Bloomberg/Getty Images; p. 23 Andrew H. Walker/ Getty Images Entertainment/Getty Images; pp. 24–25 Bruno Vincent/Getty Images News/Getty Images; p. 27 Jeff Haynes/ AFP/Getty Images; p. 29 Sam Moores/Shutterstock.com.

Library of Congress Cataloging-in-Publication Data

Quinlan, Julia J.
 Aston Martin / by Julia J. Quinlan. — First edition.
    pages cm. — (Speed machines)
 Includes index.
 ISBN 978-1-4777-0807-1 (library binding) — ISBN 978-1-4777-0986-3 (pbk.) —
 ISBN 978-1-4777-0987-0 (6-pack)
 1. Aston Martin automobile—Juvenile literature. I. Title.
 TL215.A75Q55 2014
 629.222'2—dc23
                          2012050004

Manufactured in the United States of America

CPSIA Compliance Information: Batch #S13PK8: For Further Information contact Rosen Publishing, New York, New York at 1-800-237-9932

Contents

James Bond's Car

The fictional British superspy James Bond does not drive just any cars. He drives only the sleekest, fastest, and most powerful cars. In nine different movies in this long-running series, James Bond has driven an Aston Martin. The Aston Martins featured in James Bond movies have been modified, or changed, to have exciting features that are not found in real-life sports cars. That does not mean that real-life Aston Martins are boring, though!

The DB5, shown here, is Aston Martin's most famous sports car.

The debut of the 2013 Vanquish was part of Aston Martin's marking 100 years of making cars.

Aston Martin has been around since 1913, and it is one of the oldest sports car companies in the world. Like James Bond, Aston Martin is British. Aston Martin is famous for its luxurious sports cars and for its championship racecars. Aston Martin has a long, fascinating history and has created some of the most famous sports cars, such as the DB5.

A Long History

In 1913, Lionel Martin and Robert Bamford founded Aston Martin. Bamford and Martin met each other while selling cars. They decided that they wanted to quit selling cars and start making their own. For part of the new company's name they chose Martin's last name. They added "Aston" to the name for a hill where Lionel Martin raced cars. Before the company could begin producing cars, **World War I** began, and the founders put their plans on hold to help Great Britain's war effort.

After World War I ended, the founders and different **investors** helped the company produce cars. **World War II** stopped production again. In 1947, David Brown Limited bought Aston Martin. It was under David Brown Limited's leadership that Aston Martin created the world-famous DB series. In 1972, Aston Martin entered another period of being bought and sold by different investors. Today, several companies, including Ford, share ownership of Aston Martin.

The DB6 was the model that succeeded the DB5. It was produced from 1965 until 1971.

Luxury and Quality

Aston Martin is known for being an exclusive carmaker. That means that unlike other car brands, Aston Martin does not make very many of each model. That can make getting an Aston Martin difficult. Because there are so few of each model, Aston Martins are very expensive. They can cost hundreds of thousands of dollars. For example, the 2014 Vanquish's starting price is $280,000!

Aston Martins are fast and powerful. They are also built by hand with great attention to the details.

This Aston Martin V8 Vantage belonged to Charles, Prince of Wales.

Many parts of Aston Martins, such as the fine leather interiors, are put together by hand. It takes longer to make cars this way, and because of this, fewer Aston Martins get made. That is one reason they are so expensive.

Every part of the car is carefully constructed to be of the best quality. Aston Martin uses fine woods and leathers on the interiors of its cars. These special touches make each model feel especially **luxurious**. Aston Martin gives its customers many different choices when purchasing a car. That means customers can fully **customize** their cars.

In Demand and Expensive

Since 1913, Aston Martin has been **innovating** its cars to have the best features and technology available. Aston Martin is known for having the most powerful engines, the most stylish design, and the most luxurious features. This is why Aston Martin has been the car of choice for James Bond in so many films.

One of the most expensive and exclusive Aston Martins ever made is the One 77. The Aston Martin One 77 is a supercar. Its design is futuristic, edgy, and sleek.

The One 77, shown here, was produced between 2009 and 2012.

Top: Here is a close-up view of the headlights of the One 77 at a 2011 car show. *Right*: The One 77 is a limited edition model. Limited edition means that very few of something is produced. This makes it collectible, and in the case of the One 77, very expensive!

It is a two-door, two-seat **coupe** with a long front nose and low-to-the-ground body. It has a V12 engine and a top speed of 220 mph (354 km/h.) Only 77 were produced. The Aston Martin One 77 costs almost $2 million. That price is very high, but there are car collectors who love Aston Martins so much that they are willing to pay that much for this special model!

Engineering Racecars

The most famous modern Aston Martin racecar is the DBR9. The DBR9 is based on the DB9 sports car. Much of the DBR9 is similar to the DB9, but it had to be changed quite a bit to become a racecar. Racecars have to be lower to the ground and more **aerodynamic** than sports cars. Racecars are also lighter than sports cars. Being lighter helps them **accelerate** faster. The DBR9 races in **endurance** races. In 2005, it won at the 12 Hours of Sebring, which is a 12-hour long race held in Florida.

Cars that are aerodynamic, like this DBR9, have a slim profile and sit close to the ground. That lowers the force of air pushing against the car and allows it to move faster.

Here is a DBR9 in an endurance race. Endurance racing shows how well a car performs when it is driven fast for a long period of time. Only the best-engineered cars win because this style of racing is hard on the car.

Then in 2007, the DBR9 won at the 24 Hours of Le Mans, in France. The DBR9 continued to race successfully until the end of 2011.

Aston Martin was building successful racecars right from the start. In 1922, one of the earliest Aston Martins, called the Bunny, broke ten world records at a race called the Brooklands.

Racing Legacy

Aston Martin began racing in 1922. The first race the company took part in was the French Grand Prix. Aston Martin participated in many different international races. In 1952, the company raced in the 24 Hours of Le Mans. The 24 Hours of Le Mans is the world's oldest still active endurance car race. The race is 24 hours long. For a car to drive for 24 hours straight it has to be very well **engineered**.

This V8 Vantage is racing in the 2009 24 Hours of Le Mans. In endurance races like this one, several drivers take turns racing, so that no one has to drive for too long.

Here is a DBRS9 in a 2011 endurance race in Belgium.

It is common for cars to break down or crash during the race. Many sports cars companies compete in Le Mans. Winning gives the carmaker a great reputation for its cars' performance.

Many sports car companies also race in Formula One. Aston Martin entered cars in the race in 1959 and 1960, but it never had much success. In 2009, Aston Martin announced that it planned to get back into Formula One racing, but that has not happened yet.

DB5

The DB5 is the most famous model made by Aston Martin. This was the car James Bond drove in the movie *Goldfinger*. In the 1964 movie *Goldfinger*, the DB5 had fictional accessories such as machine guns on the front bumper! *Goldfinger* made the DB5 famous. In 2010, the 1964 Aston Martin DB5 driven in the movie was sold for over $4.6 million!

The DB5 was available with either automatic or manual transmission. Automatic transmissions shift gears on their own, but manual transmissions require the driver to shift gears.

1964 DB5

Engine size	4 liters
Number of cylinders	6
Transmission	Manual or automatic
Gearbox	5 speeds (or 3-speed automatic)
0–60 mph (0–97 km/h)	7.1 seconds
Top speed	142 mph (229 km/h)

James Bond's DB5, shown here, was introduced in *Goldfinger*. It also appeared in the very opening of *Thunderball* but not in the main part of the film.

The production model of the DB5 did not have machine guns or an ejector seat. However, it was still very exciting. The DB5 was an improvement on Aston Martin's previous model, the DB4. It had a 4-liter engine, while the DB4 had a 3.7-liter engine. The DB5 was in production from 1963 until 1965. Aston Martin produced around 1,000 DB5s.

V8 Vantage

The Aston Martin V8 Vantage was introduced in 1977 and was produced until 1989. It was called "Britain's first supercar." A supercar is a sports car that is very fast, very powerful, and usually very expensive. The V8 Vantage was all of those things. The car had a top speed of 170 mph (273.5 km/h) and a V8 engine. To help the car go faster, special attention was paid to the shape of the car. It was designed to be aerodynamic and included a rear spoiler. A spoiler helps improve how a car handles when it is going fast. In 1986, Aston Martin began making a convertible version of the V8 Vantage, called the Volante.

Both the Vantage and the Volante appeared in the 1987 James Bond movie, *The Living Daylights*. In the movie, the cars had tire spikes, lasers in the hubcaps, jet engines, and many other unbelievable features.

The V8 Vantage was available only as a hardtop until 1986.

1977 V8 Vantage

Engine size	5.3 liters
Number of cylinders	8
Transmission	Manual or automatic
Gearbox	5 speeds (or 3-speed automatic)
0–60 mph (0–97 km/h)	5.2 seconds
Top speed	170 mph (273.5 km/h)

Vanquish

The Aston Martin Vanquish began as a concept car in 1998. Concept cars are different from production cars. Usually, a company will make only one concept car. Concept cars show new ideas and innovations that a company is working on. The Vanquish concept car was developed into a production car in 2001.

The 2001 Vanquish was the fastest production car ever built by Aston Martin. The Vanquish had a V12 engine and a top speed of 200 mph (321 km/h). It is very uncommon for a car to have a V12 engine.

The first generation of Vanquish, shown here, was made from 2001 until 2005.

2001 V12 Vanquish

Engine size	6 liters
Number of cylinders	12
Transmission	Manual
Gearbox	6 speeds
0–60 mph (0–97 km/h)	4.7 seconds
Top speed	200 mph (321 km/h)

The Vanquish S, shown here, was produced between 2004 and 2007.

Only the most powerful, most luxurious sports cars have such large engines. The high-performing Vanquish was perfect for James Bond, who drove this model in the 2002 film *Die Another Day*.

The original Vanquish was in production from 2001 until 2007. In 2012, Aston Martin introduced a new Vanquish. The new Vanquish has the power of the original but with updated technology, such as a lighter **chassis**.

DB9

The DB9 went into production in 2004. The DB9 is a powerful grand tourer. A grand tourer is a sports car that is designed to go for long distances at a high speed while remaining comfortable for the driver and passenger. Ian Callum designed the DB9. Callum now works as a car designer at Jaguar, another British sports car company. The DB9 was the first model built at Aston Martin's Gaydon facility in Warwickshire, England.

Here is the DB9 being introduced at a 2004 motor show in Detroit, Michigan.

The DB9 has a V12 engine and is available as coupe or a convertible. The convertible version of the DB9 is called the Volante. The DB9 is still in production today and has the same speed and power of the original. The new version of the DB9 has much of the same styling as the original, although the design has undergone some minor updates through the years.

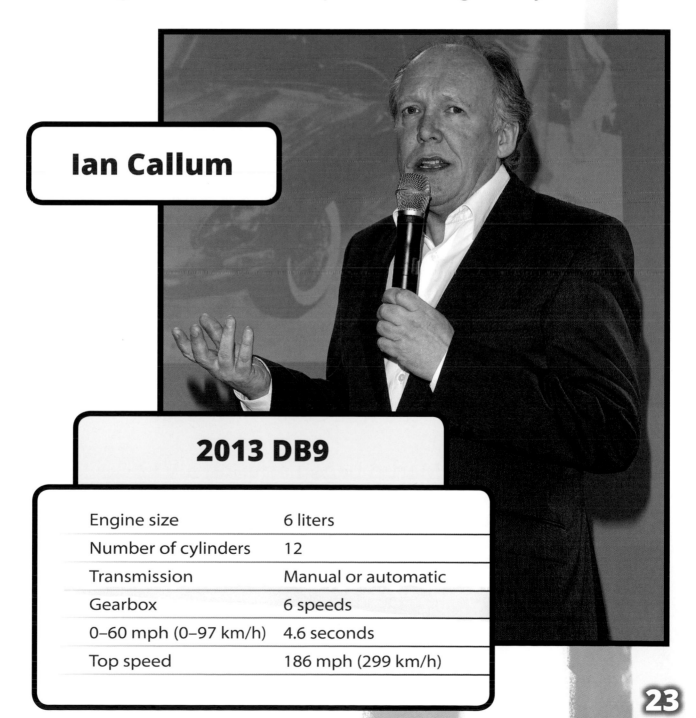

Ian Callum

2013 DB9

Engine size	6 liters
Number of cylinders	12
Transmission	Manual or automatic
Gearbox	6 speeds
0–60 mph (0–97 km/h)	4.6 seconds
Top speed	186 mph (299 km/h)

Vantage

   Aston Martin introduced the V8 Vantage in 2005. Car lovers were excited by the V8 Vantage because it was on the same level as the highly respected Porsche 911 in both performance and price. Usually, Aston Martins are much more expensive than Porsches, but the V8 Vantage was much closer in price. That meant that people who could not afford the more expensive Aston Martins now had the chance to own one. Of course, that does not mean the V8 Vantage was cheap. The 2006 V8 Vantage started at $110,000.

   In 2008, Aston Martin began offering a V12 version of the Vantage. A V12 engine is bigger than a V8 engine, but Aston Martin's engineers were able to keep the design of this Vantage relatively small, all while fitting this extremely powerful engine under the hood.

2006 V8 Vantage

Engine size	4.3 liters
Number of cylinders	8
Transmission	Manual
Gearbox	6 speeds
0–60 mph (0–97 km/h)	4.8 seconds
Top speed	175 mph (281 km/h)

The production model of the Vantage, shown here, debuted at the Geneva Motor Show in 2005. The concept version, called the AMV8, had been shown in 2003.

Rapide

The Rapide is very similar to the DB9. The biggest difference between the two models is that the Rapide has four doors while the DB9 has only two. This makes the Rapide a luxury sports sedan. The Rapide went into production in 2010. At that time, many sports car companies had begun making sedans to appeal to car buyers who wanted the option of having more than one passenger. What set the Rapide apart was that it positioned itself as a sports car first and a sedan second.

Sedans, like the Rapide, are built to be more comfortable and family-friendly than two-door sports cars.

2010 Rapide

Engine size	5.9 liters
Number of cylinders	12
Transmission	Automatic
Gearbox	6 speeds
0–60 mph (0–97 km/h)	4.7 seconds
Top speed	184 mph (296 km/h)

Here is the concept version of the Rapide, which was shown at a car show in 2006.

Aston Martin did not want to sacrifice speed, performance, or power to make their sedan. The Rapide is still a sports car. It just happens to have two extra doors.

The Rapide has the same V12 engine as the DB9. The 2010 Rapide had a top speed of 184 mph (296 km/h). Despite being bigger than the DB9, the Rapide maintains a sporty design.

100 More Years

In 2011, Aston Martin announced a new model called the Cygnet. The Cygnet is unlike any other car Aston Martin has made. It is a minicar. Minicars are very small cars made for city driving. They have lower **emissions** and get better gas mileage. Aston Martin created the Cygnet in partnership with Toyota, which is known for making small cars that produce low emissions.

The Cygnet smart car, shown here, is based on Toyota's iQ minicar. Minicars are also called city cars because they are good for getting around and parking in crowded cities.

The red version of the V12 Zagato endurance racing concept car was nicknamed "Zag." There is also a green version nicknamed "Zig."

The 2013 V12 Zagato is another new model. The V12 Zagato is an endurance racing concept car. With a roaring V12 engine and a top speed of 190 mph (305 km/h), the Zagato is an example of classic Aston Martin power with a stylish modern design. By continuing to build powerful supercars, like the Zagato, and thinking outside the box, with the Cygnet, Aston Martin will always be one of the most respected sports car companies in the world.

Comparing Aston Martins

CAR	YEARS MADE	TRANSMISSION	TOP SPEED	FUN FACT
1964 DB5	1963–1965	6-speed manual, 6-speed automatic	142 mph (228 km/h)	James Bond drove an Aston Martin DB Mark III in the *Goldfinger* novel, but it was changed to a DB5 for the movie
1977 V8 Vantage	1977–1989	5-speed manual, 3-speed automatic	170 mph (273 km/h)	The Volante used in the beginning of *The Living Daylights* was owned by one of the chairman of Aston Martin, Victor Gauntlett.
Vanquish	2001–2007	6-speed manual	200 mph (321 km/h)	The Vanquish was named third-best film car of all time for its appearance in *Die Another Day*.
2013 DB9	2004–present	6-speed manual, 6-speed automatic	183 mph (294 km/h)	A special version of the DB9 was made in 2007, in honor of Aston Martin's victory at Le Mans. It was called the DB9 LM, and only 124 were made.
2006 V8 Vantage	2006–present	6-speed manual	175 mph (281 km/h)	The racing version of the Vantage, the V12 Vantage GT3, will replace the DBRS9 racecar.
2010 Rapide	2010–present	6-speed automatic	184 mph (296 km/h)	Aston Martin CEO Ulrich Bez raced a Rapide in the 2010 24 Hours Nürburgring.

Glossary

accelerate (ik-SEH-luh-rayt) To increase in speed.

aerodynamic (er-oh-dy-NA-mik) Made to move through the air easily.

chassis (CHA-see) Parts that hold up the body of a car.

coupe (KOOP) A kind of car with two doors and a hard roof.

customize (KUS-tuh-myz) To make or change to suit a certain person.

emissions (ee-MIH-shuns) Something, such as pollution or gases, put into the air by something, such as an engine.

endurance (en-DUR-ints) Strength and the ability to go long distances without getting tired easily.

engineered (en-juh-NEER-ed) Having planned or built engines, machines, roads, and bridges.

innovating (IH-nuh-vay-ting) Creating something new.

investors (in-VES-turz) People who give money for something they hope will bring them more money later.

luxurious (lug-ZHOOR-ee-us) Very comfortable and beautiful.

World War I (WURLD WOR WUN) The war fought between the Allies and the Central powers from 1914 to 1918.

World War II (WURLD WOR TOO) The war fought by the United States, Great Britain, France, China, and the Soviet Union against Germany, Japan, and Italy from 1939 to 1945.

Index

Websites

Due to the changing nature of Internet links, PowerKids Press has developed an online list of websites related to the subject of this book. This site is updated regularly. Please use this link to access the list:
www.powerkidslinks.com/smach/aston/